Puffin Books

Penguin Books Australia Ltd, 487 Maroondah Highway, PO Box 257, Ringwood, Victoria 3134, Australia
Penguin Books Ltd, Harmondsworth, Middlesex, England
Viking Penguin, A Division of Penguin Books USA Inc., 375 Hudson Street, New York, New York 10014, USA
Penguin Books Canada Limited, 10 Alcorn Avenue, Toronto, Ontario, Canada M4V 3B2
Penguin Books (N.Z.) Ltd, 182-190 Wairau Road, Auckland 10, New Zealand

First published by Penguin Books Australia, 1993
10 9 8 7 6 5 4 3 2 1
Copyright © Alison Lester, 1993
Illustrations Copyright © Alison Lester, 1993

Typeset in Caslon by Midland Typesetters, Maryborough, Victoria
Made and printed in Hong Kong by Bookbuilders Ltd

National Library of Australia Cataloguing-in-Publication data:

Lester, Alison
I'm green and I'm grumpy.

ISBN 014 054 9684
I. Toy and movable books –Specimens. I. Title.
(Series: Open-the-door books).
A823.3

I'm Green and I'm Grumpy

ALISON LESTER

Puffin Books

It's Steve in the closet,
it's Steve we can't see.
I wonder, I wonder . . .
now what can he be?

It's Kim in the closet,
it's Kim we can't see.
I wonder, I wonder . . .
now what can she be?

I'm magic,
I'm silver,
I'm light
and I'm airy.
I'm a glittering,
twinkling,
tinkling . . .

It's Joe in the closet,
it's Joe we can't see.
I wonder, I wonder . . .
now what can he be?

I'm smooth
and I'm shiny,
and I know
such a lot.
I'm a digital,
computerized,
whirring . . .

It's Liz in the closet,
it's Liz we can't see.
I wonder, I wonder . . .
now what can she be?

It's Spike in the closet,
it's Spike we can't see.
I wonder, I wonder . . .
now what can he be?

It's Ted in the closet,
it's Ted we can't see.
I wonder, I wonder . . .
now what can he be?

I'm soft
and I'm stripy,
I'm sleepy
and fat.
I'm a
furry, purry,
fluffy . . .

It's Rose in the closet,
it's Rose we can't see.
I wonder, I wonder . . .
now what can she be?